Jellybean Books™

Pippa Mouse's House

By Betty Boegehold • Illustrated by Julie Durrell

Random House 🏠 New York

Text copyright © 1973 by Betty Boegehold. Illustrations copyright © 1998 by Julie Durrell. All rights reserved.
Originally published by Alfred A. Knopf, Inc., in a different form as "Her Mouse House" in the collections *Pippa Mouse* (1973)
and *Here's Pippa!* (1989). First Random House Jellybean Books™ edition, 1998.
ISBN: 0-679-89191-9 www.randomhouse.com/kids/
JELLYBEAN BOOKS is a trademark of Random House, Inc.
Printed in the United States of America 10 9 8 7 6 5 4 3 2 1

Rain is falling outside the mouse-hole house.

Pippa is tired of watching the rain.

"Mother, tell me a story,"
says Pippa.
   "Not yet, dear," says Mother.
"I must make the beds."
   "I will help you," says Pippa.

Slip-slap. Slip-slap. Slap-slip.
The beds are made.

"Now is it time for a story?"
asks Pippa.

"Not yet, dear," says Mother.
"Now it is time to sweep."

"I will help you," says Pippa.

Sweep. Sweep.
Brush and sweep.
The sweeping is done.

"Now is it story time?" asks Pippa.

"My goodness!" says Mother. "Look at the rain! It is coming right into our mouse-hole house."

The rain is coming down fast,
making big puddles in the green
grass, and little puddles on the floor
of the mouse-hole house.

"I will shut the door," says Pippa.
"You know we have no door,"
says Mother.
"Then I will make a door,"
says Pippa Mouse.

Pippa takes some wood
from the woodpile and puts
it all around the hole of the
mouse-hole house.

Then she takes more
pieces from the big woodpile
and nails them together.
Hammer! Hammer!
Bang! Bang! Bang!

With her strong white paws,
Pippa makes a door—a good
tight door, with a good tight
frame all around.

"There!" says Pippa.
"I made a door!"

"Thank you, Pippa Mouse,"
says Mother.
   "Now we *do* have a door,
and we *don't* have puddles.
So now it is time for a story."

Mother sits in her chair
by the warm red fire.
Pippa sits in her chair
right beside her mother.

Mother says, "Once upon
a time, a big brave mouse
found puddles coming in
her mouse-hole house."

"She took a hammer
and with a *Bing, Bang, Bin!*
kept all the water from
blowing right in!"

"Now, who's snug as
a bug in a rug? Who's the
brave dry mouse in her
new-door house?"

"Oh, Mother," says Pippa.
"I know who it is..."

"ME!"